ONCE UPON A TIME...

...On the faraway world of Eternia, twins were born to the king and queen. But soon after their birth, the little brother and sister were separated by fate.

The boy, Prince Adam, grew up on the planet Eternia. There, he learned the secrets of Castle Grayskull and that he had a great destiny. Through a magical transformation, he became He-Man, the most powerful man in the universe, and he fought on the side of goodness.

His sister, Princess Adora, was kidnapped as a baby by the wicked Hordak. She was raised by him on the planet Etheria, a world that lived in misery under the rule of Hordak and his Horde.

Only after many years were Prince Adam and Princess Adora reunited. Like Prince Adam, Adora was given a magical weapon; hers was called the Sword of Protection. Adora's Sword of Protection gave her mighty powers. With it, she was transformed into She-Ra, the Princess of Power. Her beautiful horse Spirit became Swift Wind, a flying unicorn.

Adora stayed on Etheria to work on the side of the Rebellion, which was determined to return freedom to the land. This small but dedicated band was led by Angella, queen of the Kingdom of Bright Moon.

Adora guarded the secret of She-Ra carefully. Of her many friends, only the centuries-old Madame Razz and little Kowl knew who She-Ra, the Princess of Power, really was.

One other possessed the secret of She-Ra. High atop a mountain was the Crystal Castle, a shining palace that was She-Ra's special place. At the bottom of a mysterious pool in the castle dwelled the spirit of Light Hope, She-Ra's powerful friend.

No one but She-Ra could see this wonderful castle. And only on the day that all Etheria was free would Light Hope's secrets be known to all.

It was for that day, when goodness would reign again over Etheria, that She-Ra pledged her power.

Everything but Happiness

Written by Bryce Knorr

Illustrated by Harry J. Quinn and James Holloway

Creative Direction by Jacquelyn A. Lloyd

Design Direction by Ralph E. Eckerstrom

A GOLDEN BOOK

Western Publishing Company, Inc.
Racine, Wisconsin 53404

Library of Congress Catalog Card Number 84-062814
ISBN 0-307-16112-9
A B C D E F G H I J

Classic™ Binding U.S. Patent #4,408,780
Patented in Canada 1984.
Patents in other countries issued or pending.
R. R. Donnelley and Sons Company

"Whee!" Glimmer said. She skated to a shaky stop. "Thanks for inviting us, Frosta. Winter is so much fun!"

"Winter?" Frosta, the Ice Empress, laughed. "This is summer in the Kingdom of Snows. But we know Bright Moon is warmer. That's why we made this special skating rink for all of you. You can skate and keep warm at the same time."

Adora skated a graceful figure eight on the ice.
"How do you do it, Frosta?" she asked. "Those hot springs look very warm.
Why doesn't the ice melt?"
"It's Frosta's magic," Kowl said. He skated by backwards. "That's why she
can live here. She has power over the cold."
"Kowl is right," Frosta said. "I make the cold do what I want."

"There is a legend," Kowl said. "Long ago, Etheria's greatest wizard was named Endor."

Then Kowl told them a poem:

"When winter ice is warm,
 Or summer freezes cold,
 You know Endor's magic,
 Has you in its hold!"

Kowl didn't see a hole in the ice. He skated right over a blast of hot steam. Into the air he flew!

"I like steam baths," Kowl said. "But that is too much steam!"

A worried look lined Frosta's face.

"I'm sorry, Kowl," she said. "Something is wrong. I can't keep the ice cold!"

Adora felt danger. "Frosta needs She-Ra's help," she thought.

"Kowl is all wet," Adora said. "I'll get him a towel."

Adora made sure she was out of sight.

"By the honor of Grayskull," she said.

"I AM SHE-RA!"

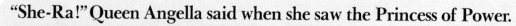

"She-Ra!" Queen Angella said when she saw the Princess of Power. "Am I glad you are here. We need your power."

The queen told She-Ra what had happened.

"That's why we came on this visit," Angella continued. "Frosta told me that strange things were happening."

"Look!" Glimmer said. "Frosta is turning blue!"

"It's so cold," Frosta said. "Why do I feel so cold?"

She-Ra touched Frosta. A golden glow covered them both.

"You are not sick," She-Ra said. "Someone is taking your magic power!"

The blue left Frosta's face.

"You'll feel better now," She-Ra said. "But I must go. I'll return if you need me."

"I'm all right," Frosta told the others. "Look. The hole in the ice is frozen again."

Adora came back with a towel. "Kowl can't blame the ice now if he falls," she joked.

"There you are," Kowl said with a wink. Only he and Madame Razz knew that Adora was She-Ra. "I thought you would never get here."

Kowl flew into the air to dry off. The water dripped on his friends, not the towel.

"Oh Kowl!" Frosta laughed. "You make me forget my problems. But I wonder. What is wrong with me?"

"Your power comes from magic," Adora said. "Maybe magic is the thing taking it away."

"You are right, Adora," Angella said. "We need Castaspella. You and Glimmer go to Mystacor. Bring back Castaspella right away!"

Glimmer flashed about on a beam of light. She was excited by adventure. "Don't use up all your light power," Angella warned. "You have a long trip."

Adora and Glimmer rode as fast as they could. Soon, they came to a fork in the road.

"Let's try a shortcut," Glimmer said. Adora agreed. But soon she was sorry. They were lost in a blinding snowstorm.

Through the falling flakes, Adora and Glimmer saw something. They could not believe it.

"It looked like a deer," Glimmer said. "A deer with golden horns!"

"I saw it, too," Adora said. "Could it be real?"

Glimmer chased the deer, and Adora followed. Suddenly, they were in a beautiful forest. The snow was gone! Instead, a warm sun shone.

"I have never seen a place like this!" Glimmer said.

"Neither have I," Adora agreed. "But something feels wrong. Those silver birds in the trees. They are..."

The birds flew to the ground. They changed into soldiers. The princesses were trapped!

"Touch your staff!" Adora cried. "Get away!" But Glimmer had used all the power in her magic staff.

"You can't get away," a guard said. "No one leaves the land of Endor. And you won't need your staff and your sword."

The guards took them to a silvery castle. Inside a great hall, they met Endor, the master of the castle.

"Forgive my guards," he said. "I have few visitors. How did you get here?"

Adora told him what had happened. "We must leave now," she said. "May we have our horses and our sword and wand back?"

"Oh, don't think of that now," Endor said. "You have plenty of time. First, you must meet my daughter. This is Astral."

Adora and Glimmer met a lovely but shy-looking girl. Astral looked at both of them very closely.

"You're both so lovely. You look like princesses," Astral said. "And you're real!"

"I hope so," Adora said. "Why do you ask?"

Endor stepped between them. "You can talk later," he said. "Now, you need clothes."

Endor clapped his hands. Beautiful dresses appeared. "Of course, you will need jewelry, too," he said. In an instant, he had produced wonderful necklaces and rings.

"Enjoy these gifts," Endor said. "I want you to have a very pleasant visit."

Adora and Glimmer shared a beautiful room. "I never saw anything like this on Etheria," Adora said. "And Endor certainly is generous. But I thought he was only a legend."

"That's what everyone says," Glimmer said. "According to the story, one day he disappeared. He and his wife and daughter were never seen again. I wonder if we will ever see our friends again."

"Of course we will," Adora said. "I hope."

Endor gave Adora and Glimmer more presents. But he would not let them leave.

"Astral needs friends to play with," he said. "Please, stay a little longer."

"We have no choice," Adora said angrily. "How can we leave when your guards follow us wherever we go?"

"That's for your own good," Endor snapped back. "Now, please, go and play with my daughter."

Adora and Glimmer liked Astral very much. They told her many stories. Astral liked the stories about She-Ra best. Soon, she was playing She-Ra all over the castle.

"She-Ra must be very beautiful," Astral said. "I wish I could grow up to be beautiful."

"You will," Adora said. "You will be a beautiful woman before you know it."

Astral began to cry. "No, I won't," she said. "I will never grow up!"

Endor's daughter ran away. She came back later. But she would not tell Adora and Glimmer what was wrong.

"What is the matter?" Adora asked. "We can't help unless you tell us."

But Astral would not tell them why she was unhappy.

Adora watched Astral playing She-Ra. She got an idea.
"Here is how we can escape," she told Glimmer. "Astral pretends she is
She-Ra. Why don't we pretend we are guards?"
"But we would need uniforms," Glimmer said. So they decided to ask
Astral for help one last time.

"Won't you get us two guard uniforms?" Adora asked Astral. "If we could go home, maybe we could bring She-Ra here to see you."

"Well," Astral said. "My father and I will be alone. You will come back to see us, won't you?"

"We will do our best," Adora answered. "We want to help your father. He is a very powerful man. But he does not seem happy."

"I will help you," Astral said. "You are my friends."

Astral found the smallest guard uniforms she could. They just fit Adora and Glimmer. No one stopped them when Astral took them to the stables. They found their horses, the Sword of Protection and Glimmer's wand. "Goodbye," Adora said. "We will come back and bring She-Ra with us."

Adora and Glimmer rode hard to get away from Endor's castle. They raced through the front gate and were back in the cold Kingdom of Snows! "Look. Back there," Adora said. "Where the castle was. It's a patch of falling snow."

Adora rode Spirit into the snow. She was back at Endor's castle. The snow patch was the portal to Endor's land. And Endor's guards were headed right toward her!

Adora remembered Kowl's poem:
"When winter ice is warm,
  Or summer freezes cold,
  You know Endor's magic,
  Has you in its hold!"
"This really must be the Endor of legend!" Adora thought. "But where
is his wife?"
  She rode back to Glimmer.
"Get away from here quickly," Adora said. "I'll meet you back at Castle
Bright Moon. Please go. I don't have time to explain."
  Glimmer was full of questions. But she did what her friend asked. When
Glimmer was gone, Adora raised her Sword of Protection.

"By the honor of Grayskull," she said.

"I AM SHE-RA!"

Endor's surprised guards saw She-Ra racing toward them. They blocked the road. Swift Wind flew into the air. She landed at the castle.

"You won't get past this!" Endor said. Lightning flashed from his fingers. She-Ra's Sword of Protection stopped the bolts.

"No, Father!" Astral yelled. "This is She-Ra. She has come to be my friend."

Endor folded his arms. She-Ra put away her Sword of Protection.

"It is an honor to meet you, Endor," She-Ra said. "You *are* a legend. But why do you fight me? Why do you take Frosta's power?"

"You are powerful, also, She-Ra," Endor said. "You have discovered my secret." A tear fell from his eye.

The castle shook slightly. "I have no choice," Endor explained. "I *must* take Frosta's power."

"Once I was happy," he said. "I had a beautiful wife and daughter. I had everything I wanted.

"But my wife became sick. I knew she would die. So I cast a spell."

Endor waved his hands. They went deep inside his castle. Before them lay a beautiful sleeping woman.

"She is my wife," he said. "I had to save her. So I stopped time. I hoped one day to make her better. But I could not.

"I tried to give Astral everything. What you see here is not real. My magic made it all. But each year, I need more power to keep the spell alive."

"So you took Frosta's power," She-Ra said. Endor nodded. "Maybe I can help you."

She touched Endor's wife. Both were filled with a golden glow.

"I . . . I cannot do it," She-Ra said sadly. She fell back. "I have failed."

But the woman began to move. "Look!" shouted Astral. She-Ra's healing power had worked!

"Thank you for saving my wife," Endor said. "But I cannot repay your kindness. I still need Frosta's power."

"But why?" She-Ra asked. "You don't need this magic castle anymore."

"Yes, we do," Endor said. "We are trapped in an island of time."

"I stopped time a thousand years ago," Endor said. "If we left our island of time, we would become a thousand years old."

"But you are a legend," She-Ra said. "Can't you go to the Land of Legends?"

"No," Endor said. "Not even I am that strong."

"But She-Ra has great power," Astral said. "Maybe she can help."

"My Sword of Protection is strong," She-Ra said. "The power of two worlds flows through it. The power is yours."

"Maybe there is a spell," Endor said.

Endor began to whisper. His family held their hands together. "Place your Sword of Protection on our hands, She-Ra," Endor said. "And wish us good luck."

The castle began to fade. "It's working!" Endor shouted. "You must leave, She-Ra. Hurry! Or you will be trapped in the Land of Legends."

"Goodbye, She-Ra," Astral said. "Thank you for making us a family again. I will never forget you."

She-Ra ran from the castle. She hopped on Swift Wind. Everything around them swirled as time came unstuck. Swift Wind took off.

Suddenly, She-Ra was in a snow-covered field. All was quiet. "We made it, Swift Wind," she said.

At Castle Bright Moon, Adora told Glimmer everything. Well, almost everything.

"...And She-Ra's power helped them get to the Land of Legends," Adora told her friend.

"Endor's castle surely was nice," Glimmer sighed. "He had so much. It was like a dream."

"But even a beautiful dream can be a nightmare," Adora said. "You can't buy love, or friends. Endor had everything—but happiness."

Angella came into her daughter's room. It was a mess.

"Glimmer!" she said. "Please clean up this room right away!"

"We sure could use Endor's magic now," Glimmer said.

"I'll help you," Adora said. "The only magic that gets rid of chores is doing them."

THE END

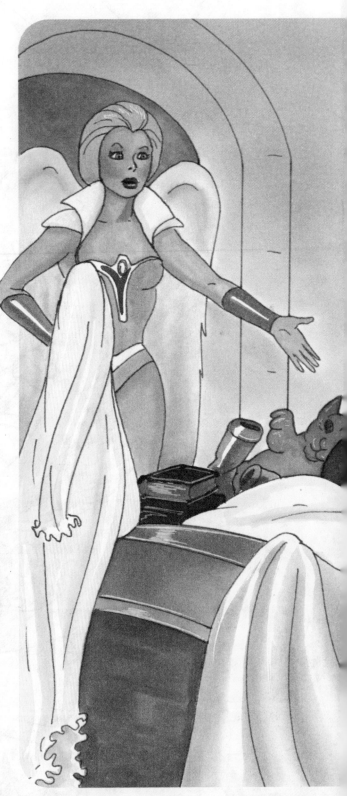